TREETURE CREATURES

AND

FLOWERBUDS

Oaky

the

Oak Leaf

I would like to dedicate this book to my wonderful mum and dad,
Sean and Anne Stapleton.
I miss you and my love always.

To my patient and "yes I am listening", husband Jim,
and my amazing children, Sarah, Rose and John.

Special thanks to Mary Bass and Pete True.

Published in the United Kingdom by:

Blue Falcon Publishing
The Mill, Pury Hill Business Park,
Alderton Road, Towcester
Northamptonshire NN12 7LS
Email: books@bluefalconpublishing.co.uk
Web: www.bluefalconpublishing.co.uk

A CIP record of this book is available from the British Library.

First printed June 2021
ISBN 97819127652324

TREETURE CREATURES

AND

FLOWERBUDS

Oaky
the
Oak Leaf

Marian Hawkins

The breeze sways Oaky Oak Leaf as he's hanging by a thread,

then he drops, floating gracefully, down to the flowerbed.

"Well hi there, I apologise for my alarming landing!"

Oaky grins at Daisy, who is no longer upstanding.

Daisy says, "Hello you!" but there is no time to chat,

the strong wind swirls and Oaky grabs onto his crown-like hat.

Oaky lands, "Hi Alder, I'm lost; are you from my tree?

I blew in on the wind; do you think you could help me?"

"My tree is used to make boats, in the water it is good.

Alder trees make paper; did you know that comes from wood?

They grow cone-like fruit and there are no lobes on it's leaves.

Their blooms make dye for fairies' clothes, so says an old belief.

The fairies hide within my leaves, disguised by darkest green."

Then Alder laughs, "If you look hard, sometimes they can be seen!"

"How nice to meet you, Alder, but you are not from my tree."

Alder agrees, "That's right, the alder tree belongs to me."

From the corner of one eye, Oaky glimpses something move.

Perhaps it was a fairy. Could be difficult to prove.

Jolted from his thoughts, the ground beneath him starts to shake,

As a tractor rumbles close, Oaky shouts, "Please use your brake!"

Too late! It rolls along with Oaky sticking to the wheel.

As it splashes and it sploshes, Oaky goes round with a squeal.

Dizzy Oaky, glad to stop, is now high on a hill.

"I feel a little wobbly and I cannot stand still."

Ah, a new friend! "Hello Rowan, are you from my tree?
I've been spun round by a tractor; please could you help me?"
"Greetings Oaky, I'm from the wizard's tree by Celtic name,
I protect people from witches, for that is my tree's fame!
Rowan's bark is slightly ridged and coloured silver grey,
and it produces white flowers that will bloom in early May.
It has lots of species, and it's fruits are scarlet red.
Myth says I expel dark magic that all witches dread!"
"So good to meet you Rowan, but you are not from my tree."
"No Oaky, you're right, the Rowan tree belongs to me."

A bright balloon floats by and Oaky's caught upon its strings.

Flying high and taking in the view, he sways and swings.

The red balloon drifts down and Oaky drops into a garden.

"That was fun! Oh hello Buttercup, I beg your pardon."

Buttercup stands proud and bright with petals shiny yellow.

A soft voice says, "Okay, but maybe next time you could bellow?"

"Yes, I will," says Oaky. "Now that I'm off that balloon,

goodbye, I hope to get back to my oak tree sometime soon!"

Oaky meets with Holly next. "Hi! Are you from my tree?
I've floated in on a balloon; perhaps you could help me?"
"Don't come too close, I'm spiky, although I might look cute.
At Christmas time I'm used for decoration, as I'm a beaut!"
Holly smiles, "My red berries are great food for the birds,
and the evergreen leaves are eaten by deer in their herds.
Legend says bad luck will come to those who cut me down.
But I'm sure you want to get home, I can see that from your frown."
"Nice to meet you Holly, but you are not from my tree."
"I'm a prickly one; the Holly tree belongs to me."
"I have been blown, squashed and rolled into the muddy ground.
Up and down, made dizzy, but some great friends I have found.
The strong wind blew me far away from where I'm meant to be."
Poor Oaky sighs, "How will I make it home to my oak tree?"

A quiet voice says, "Hello there, have you lost your way?"
It's Bluebell, looking lovely in the bright light of midday.
"Hi there Bluebell, yes, you're right, I am a touch adrift.
To get back to my mighty oak would give me such a lift."
A spider's web tickles Oaky causing him to giggle,
and so he heads off on his way after a little wriggle.
"Nice to meet you, Bluebell, thanks for showing me the way.
Your flower really does put on the most awesome display!"

A big gust of wind comes and Oaky wishes, "Take me back!"
Oaky's home; he hits the mighty grey trunk with a whack.
In the world of trees, the oak is thought to be the king.
The early flush of light green leaves start to shoot in spring.
Oak grows very tall and heavy branches fill its crown;
some live to be a thousand years old, if they don't fall down.
On long stalks they grow acorns that sit in little cups;
they fall down to the ground, where many creatures scoff them up,
like pigeons, deer, pigs and mice, even the odd duck,
leftovers might sprout and may grow with a little luck.
As autumn comes, Oaky turns a lovely reddish brown,
waiting for the spring, amongst his friends, Oaky lies down.

"My adventure is complete, and it really has been fun.
I have met some great buds, leaves and trees, each a special one."
When winter's passed, new growth will begin peeking through the earth,
signs of better weather coming, for springtime's new birth.
So now let's get outside and see which ones you can find.
Look after all our buds and trees, and make sure to be kind!

The Importance of Trees

Trees take in carbon dioxide (co2) and change it into oxygen (o2) for us to breathe. This process is called photosynthesis. As a result of this, trees are vital. Therefore, the more we have, the more we can slow the effects of global warming. With enough light, the tree absorbs the co2 and water, changing it into glucose and oxygen. This ensures our atmosphere stays oxygen rich. Our wonderful trees can also improve the air quality by catching airborne particles of pollution which, can reduce smog levels.

There are many reasons trees are important. Here are just a few!

Trees **clean** the air.   They provide **shelter** for wildlife.

They enhance areas with their **beauty**.

They **stabilise** soil.   They offer **shade** and wind breaks.

They help with **flood** control.   They help with **noise** reduction.

They are great **fun** to climb..   They **produce** oxygen.

They supply us with wonderful **food**.

In the UK only 13% of our land is covered by forests. In comparison to other European countries this is low.

"Wow, aren't our trees clever? We need to plant more, however."

Oaky found his tree.
Can you help the others find theirs?

Holly   Rowan   Alder

Tree truths:

Oak
Over 500 species.
Acorns - slow growing but long living.
Can live for up to 1,000 years.
Makes furniture, floorboards and good firewood.

Holly
Said to be bad luck to cut holly down.
Spiked glossy leaves.
Red berries.
Evergreen foliage.
Found in oak or beech woods.

Rowan
Likes higher altitudes.
Leaf - feather-like appearance.
According to Celtic belief, planted to
protect from witches.
Celtic name, fid na ndruad, means
wizard's tree.
Protects against dark magic.

Alder
Wood used for making lock gates,
clogs or pier pilings.
A past source of charcoal used in gunpowder.
Grow in marshlands, and help contain erosion
on riversides.
Dye from the leaves used for fairy clothes,
according to ancient belief.

Weird and Wonderful
The Socotra Dragon Tree

This tree is found on an island called Socotra. This can be found in the Arabian Sea. The island is part of Yemen. Dragon Tree is an evergreen, meaning it keeps its leaves all year round. In ancient times people called this tree the Dragon Blood Tree. This is because it has a dark red paste.
The resin is used in medicines that help with digestive health, for instance, if you had a bad tummy.

The Dragon Tree has adapted itself to be able to live in very
dry conditions, where there isn't much soil. Its umbrella-like
crown provides shade, which reduces evaporation.
This allows it to survive with access to little water.
The root of the Dragon Tree also has its uses, such as a
stimulant in toothpastes and as relief for painful joints.

An Oak Through the Seasons

Spring, summer, autumn, winter; seasons come and go.
Marvellous changes take place, nature's wondrous show.
Spring is our first season, bringing new growth for the year.
On the bare branches of winter, young green shoots now appear.
Oak's catkin flowers pollinate to let the acorns grow.
Young oaks don't grow fruit; they must be 40 years old or so.
Early summer sees oak full of leaves, a bright, light green,
but just a few weeks later on, a darker shade is seen.
A canopy of shade protects from sun's strong, beaming rays.
Dappled light twirls on the grass beneath on summer days.
As the leaves change colour, we know autumn's on its way.
Golden yellows, reds and browns are striking on display.
Oak draws pigment from the leaves and sends it to the root.
This nourishes the oak for when it comes back into fruit.
As one by one leaves flutter down, a sign that winter's near,
fallen leaves crunch underfoot, a pleasant sound to hear.
They rot down into minerals returning to the earth,
strengthening the oak, preparing for springtime's new birth.
Above, a canopy of twigs and branches fill the space,
as its bark acts like a blanket, and leaves surround the base.
The oak is well adapted, coping with each season's weather.
It deals with fierce sun, heavy rains, hail and snow... whatever.
Spring, summer, autumn, winter; seasons come and go.
Marvellous changes taking place, nature's wondrous show.

Summer

Autumn

Spring

Winter

Treeture Creatures and Flowerbuds
Book 2 – Willow the Willow Leaf

It's Willow's turn for an adventure this time, as the little leaf finds himself washed downstream and makes many new friends as he tries to find his way back to where he belongs.

Available to buy from Amazon, Waterstones and Foyles.

Treeture Creatures and Flowerbuds
Book 3 – Beech the Beech Leaf

When an unsuspecting beech leaf is whisked away on a ball, she learns a lot about the trees and flowers that surround her as she bounces, floats and squelches her way back to her beloved beech tree!

Available to buy from Amazon, Waterstones and Foyles.

Also Available
The Tree Trail Swatch Booklets

Heading out to the park?
Take Oaky and his friends with you on your adventure!
Pop the tree trail booklet in your pocket and see how many
trees and leaves you can spot on your day out! The booklet
will help you identify which leaf is from which tree.
Take pictures and share what you find on your day out with
us on Instagram @treeture_creatures_flowerbuds.
ISBN – 9781912765-40-9

Also Available
The Flower Trail Swatch Booklets

Let's go outside!
Take bluebell and her friends with you on your adventure!
Pop the flower trail booklet in your pocket and see how
many wild flowers you can spot on your day out! The booklet
will help you identify wild flowers whilst learning interesting
facts. Take pictures and share what you find on your day
out with us on Instagram @treeture_creatures_flowerbuds.

ISBN – 9781912765-41-6

Lightning Source UK Ltd.
Milton Keynes UK
UKHW050354010721
386407UK00002B/117

9 781912 765324